This is the story of two young boys who,
after overcoming great hardship and adversity,
became members of the court of Her Royal Majesty,
the Queen of England.

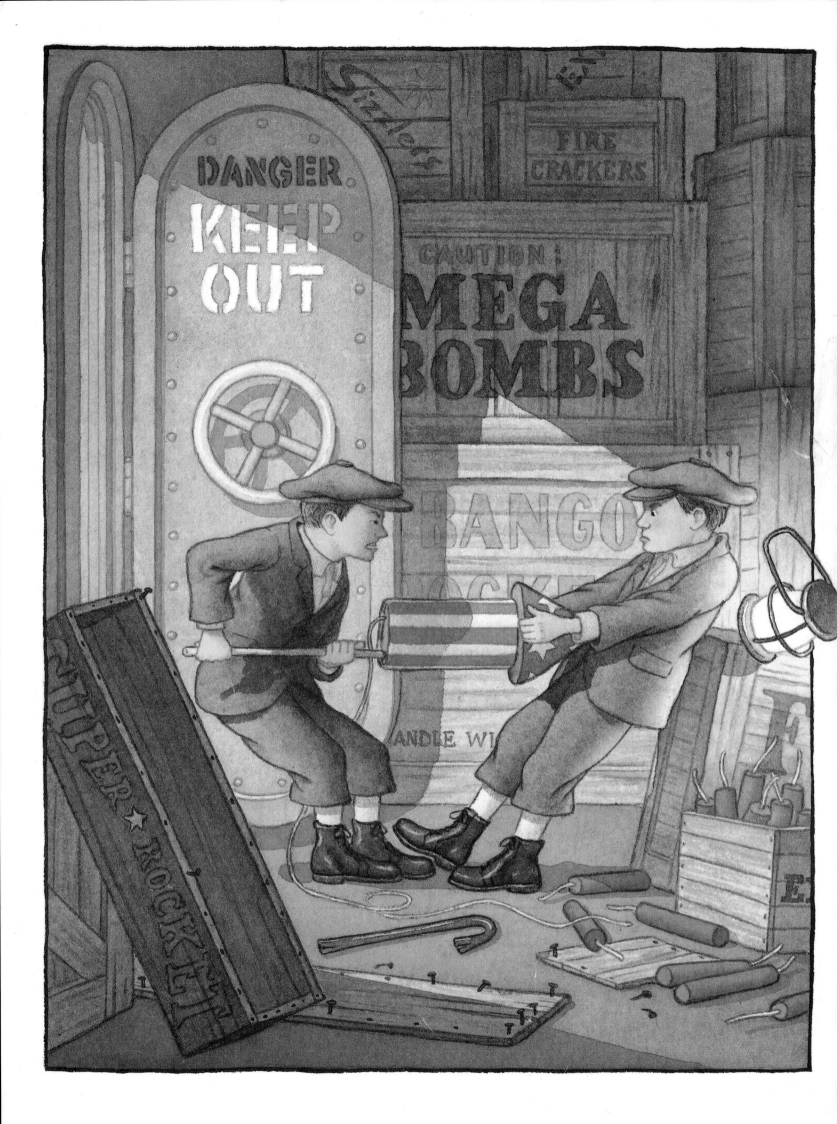

Oh, Brother

story *by* **Arthur Yorinks**
pictures by **Richard Egielski**

Michael di Capua Books
Farrar · Straus · Giroux New York

For Adrienne, Murray, and Mary
A.Y.

For my brother, Bob
R.E.

It was a sorry accident at sea many years ago that caused
Milton and Morris, twins from England, to be left all alone in the world,
fending as best they could.

Washed up in New York, shuffled from orphanage to orphanage, from one wayward home to another, the poor boys were not spared the harshness of life. Still, they always had each other, to give to each other comfort and consolation.

"You stink!" Milton would say to Morris.

"So do you!" Morris would answer Milton.

Well, perhaps their brotherly love had not quite bloomed. Anyway, they never separated. Indeed, one night they both escaped from Rotten's Home for Lost Boys and together joined the circus.

Under the big top, Milton and Morris at first groomed elephants. But opportunity soon fell their way and they were promoted to the trapeze.

What glamour. What fame. What costumes!

On opening night, THE TINY TIMS, as they were called, swung high above the center ring. The drum rolled. The spotlight narrowed.

And Morris was yelling. "Catch *you*? I'm not catching you!"
"So don't! Do *I* care?" Milton replied.

They never stopped arguing. Even as the firemen carried them down and the circus owner bellowed "You're fired!" they continued their spirited discussion.

Thrown back to the unforgiving streets, the boys tried selling apples. Unfortunately, this didn't last long either.

In a debate over what to charge, they managed to lose their entire stock of fruit.

Well, ever determined to make good, the brothers next tried singing songs for a nickel. Instantly, they were barraged with requests.

Requests to leave.

Ah, fate can be so cruel and bitter. And empty stomachs can make crime a sweet temptation. Milton and Morris became pickpockets.

One day they attempted to steal a watch from a chubby old man. But, being gifted in neither height nor thievery, they got themselves tangled in the man's suspenders.

This was serious. Prison loomed. But the old man never called the police. He just walked down the street, twins dangling, and roared with laughter.

"Hey, baldy, let go of us!" Morris shouted.

"Yeah, c'mon tubby, let us go!" Milton yelled.

But the old man said, "Boys, I'm taking you home to give you a proper roof over your heads."

And Nathan — that was the man's name — was more than true to his word. He clothed them. And fed them. And even taught them his trade, custom tailoring.

You'd think with such a happy turn in their fortunes the twins would have counted their blessings. They did not.

They bit the furniture and spilt their milk and generally gave Nathan nothing but trouble.

Yet Nathan didn't mind. He was glad to have the company in his old age. "They're young and what's the harm in that," he thought. For really he loved the two boys as if they were his own sons.

And such a powerful love as that must have penetrated the boys' thick skins. For one day Nathan's heart failed, and Milton and Morris realized at once what kindness they had lost and they cried and hugged each other and didn't argue for days.

But now, alone again, what were they to do? Face the streets and a life of woe and misery?

No. They had an idea.

They disguised themselves as little old men and claimed to be Nathan's relatives from the old country. They took in new trade and worked hard and became the most magnificent tailors.

People from all over, even Connecticut, came to Milton and Morris for clothes. The Morgans, the Rockefellers, Fred Astaire. Everyone.

One afternoon, Mrs. Guggenheim brought her husband to the shop.

"We're leaving for England tomorrow to visit with the Queen, and my husband needs the finest suit you make. Can you do it?" she asked.

The tailor twins shrugged. "Of course," they said, and immediately went to work.

Measuring. Cutting. Sewing. Pressing. By the end of the day
Mr. Guggenheim tried on his new suit. The fit was extraordinary.
"He never looked so good," Mrs. Guggenheim exclaimed. "What
pleats! You two simply must come with us to meet the Queen."

How life turns. There were Milton and Morris, in England, being introduced to the royal family. They were given a splendid welcome by the entire court. Everyone, that is, except for the gardener and his wife, nanny to the young Prince of Wales. She eyed the twins up and down and suddenly spoke out.

"Impostors! Impostors! You're not old men!" she screamed. "You're devils, you're scoundrels, you're...our children! Miltie, Murray — oh, it's a miracle!"

It was. For on that sad Atlantic voyage the twins' parents were rescued and brought back to England, thinking they had lost their children forever.

Her Majesty, displaying infinite wisdom and fine sartorial taste, knighted

the twins Sir Milton and Sir Morris, Master Tailors to the Prince of Wales.

And, to this day, who do you think makes his suits?